RELENTLESS LORD

❧

AMY SANDAS

Copyright © 2021 by Amy Sandas

All rights reserved.

No part of this book may be reproduced in any form or by any electronic or mechanical means, including information storage and retrieval systems, without written permission from the author, except for the use of brief quotations in a book review.

❦ Created with Vellum

DEDICATION

To December Gephart, my friend, critique partner, and an amazing writer. Thanks for all the honesty and encouragement, the brainstorming sessions, and the late-night talks over bottles of wine. You rock!
And to the Wausau area Wisconsin RWA group, a wonderful bunch of writers who continue to inspire and motivate me.

THE REGENCY ROGUES SERIES

Rogue Countess

Reckless Viscount

Rebel Marquess

Relentless Lord (novella)

CHAPTER 1

Lancashire, England 1815

Hannah Walpole had never in her life faced such a unique and exasperating challenge. And that was saying something since she had been in some harrowing situations in her twenty years of life.

If there was one thing she had learned since coming to England two years ago, it was that a lady must maintain decorum at all times. Even when her garter twisted so badly it pinched the sensitive skin at the back of her thigh. Hannah initially thought the pinched garter would resolve itself and continued on her way toward the grand drawing room where everyone was gathering to start off the weeklong party. Unfortunately, with each added stride, the discomfort increased.

By the time she decided to do something, she had reached the main level of the country house. Guests milled about in every direction as they greeted each other and began the endless socializing that would be expected during the visit. The idea of traversing back through so many curious gazes while pretending not to feel the agonizing pinch made the trek back to her guest bedroom seem like a journey of a thousand miles.

She would never make it.

Following one of her father's oft-repeated rules—*If your chosen path becomes impassable, simply change direction*—Hannah looked about for other options.

That was when she recalled the location of a water closet along one of the hallways extending from the rear of the grand hall. Sidling around the growing crowd, Hannah had made her way one painful step after another toward the dimly lit corridor. The tour of the house she had been given earlier in the day had been extensive and she was fairly certain she remembered the way to the water closet.

She was wrong.

In a house like this, cobbled together over generations of additions and remodels, she soon got turned around by the myriad junctions and secondary hallways that branched off in every direction. Finally acknowledging her predicament, and frankly, because the pain of her garter would not allow another step, Hannah stopped and assessed her situation.

Hannah Walpole, daughter of two of the most experienced and extensive explorers of the African continent, had gotten herself lost in a house.

Certainly, it was a palatial estate made up of various wings and towers and other added structures that spread out over several acres.

But still…it was a house.

She stood in the middle of a short hallway, really just a passage that connected two other longer hallways, both of which Hannah had already been down with absolutely no evidence of a water closet. She was not opposed to finding an alternative room to use, but that meant she now had to retrace her path. And at the moment, she did not think she could move another step.

To test it, she gently shifted her weight. There was an immediate tightening of the garter and a quick gasp of pain.

"Bloody ridiculous," she muttered to herself, then quickly glanced around.

Thank goodness, there was no one about to hear her crude curse or witness her humiliating degradation. As the thought finished in her mind, Hannah realized an added benefit of that fact. She stilled to listen for any nearby movement.

She was quite alone.

After only the briefest hesitation, she grasped her skirts and flipped them up to her hip as she reached down the back of her leg for the offending clasp. The farther she reached, the more strain was put on her leg and the tighter the damned thing pinched.

She muttered another furious curse and straightened with a grunt of pain.

"May I be of some assistance?" Though the words offered aid, the deep masculine tone suggested amusement.

Hannah dropped her skirts over her legs and whipped her head toward the voice. The swift movement caused another sting of pain and another sharp inhalation The lighting was dim in the short passageway, but it was enough for Hannah to determine she now stood in the presence of an extremely attractive gentleman.

She guessed him to be in his late twenties. He held his gloves in his hands, but other than that, he was dressed at the height of gentlemanly fashion in elegant black breeches and a dove-gray coat over an emerald-colored waistcoat. He had thick black hair, a hard angled jaw, and a broad forehead.

His roguish expression struck Hannah most disconcertingly, because despite his attempt at casting his features into a solemn expression, he did not quite manage it. There was a rather exaggerated downward pull on his mouth, suggesting he was doing everything he could to hold back his laughter. As if in an attempt to compensate for the rebellion of his mouth, he had his dark eyebrows drawn low over a striking gaze.

It was in those eyes that Hannah became momentarily lost.

Eyes that continued to stare at her curiously from the short distance separating them.

Eyes such a vivid green beneath the sweep of black lashes they reminded her of the lush vegetation that spread along the Nile during growing season.

Eyes that laughed despite his solemn expression.

She had heard tales of eyes like his.

Hannah stiffened abruptly, sending another shot of pain through her leg.

She scanned his features. Indeed, they matched a description she had heard spoken of numerous times in the past. Hannah suspected this was the very rake who had seduced and rejected her poor cousin two years ago. And, if rumors were to be believed, at least a dozen other young women just like her.

Of all the people she could have encountered at this moment, it would be her luck that it should be a notorious scoundrel known for ruining innocent young women.

"Excuse me," she muttered, all her cousin's warnings about this man tumbling over themselves through her thoughts. "I should go."

She would be better served to take her chances in the labyrinth-like hallways than stand another minute with this man. She turned to head in the opposite direction. In her haste, she forgot about the situation with her garter. The fierce twisting motion of her body as she spun around caused the thing to catch even more of her flesh in its grip.

Her breath hissed between her teeth and she closed her eyes tight against the prick of tears. How humiliating to be brought low by an incessant piece of lady's underwear.

"You are obviously in distress," the green-eyed scoundrel said as he came toward her. "Allow me to help."

"No. I am quite all right." Hannah lifted her hand to him in a gesture to keep him at bay.

There had to be a way out of this.

He obeyed her silent request and stopped his advance. His gaze was open and direct as he stared back at her. After a moment, he tipped his head and widened his lips in a smile.

"I understand your reticence in accepting my assistance, but you may have no other choice. From what I can tell, your problem lies somewhere beneath your skirts."

Hannah narrowed her gaze. He was no gentleman at all if he would speak so plainly about her person.

When she did not reply, he arched his brows in question. "Unless, there is some other reason you felt a need to throw them up."

Hannah scowled. Now that was definitely not a gentlemanly thing to say. And if she were in her right mind, she would have come up with something terribly scathing to say in reply.

As it was, she was still a bit stunned by the smile he had flashed at her. The man was ridiculously handsome. And really, did a man that attractive need such a potent gaze?

He took a couple steps closer, spreading his hands to his sides. "I can help. Tell me what is causing your pain."

She eyed him warily. She would be stupid to trust a man with his reputation.

"Do you have a choice?" he asked, a note of reckless challenge in his tone.

Did she?

Another of her father's rules came to mind.

Not all challenges one may face can be predicted. Outside assistance may occasionally be required.

Surely, that could not apply to her current situation.

But the rogue with laughing eyes was right. What choice did she have? The longer she remained here, the sooner her absence would be noted. And Hannah had no wish to incite her uncle's wrath.

After a slow breath, during which she questioned her sanity, Hannah replied, "The clasp of my garter is pinching my skin. I cannot release it without making it worse."

"Then you are in luck, sweet damsel, for I happen to know my way around lady's garters quite well. I shall have you freed in no time."

Before she could think twice or attempt to stop him, he took two long strides to her side and lowered himself to one knee. He smiled up at her with his hand hovering over her skirts; those green eyes boldly meeting hers.

"May I?" he asked. His voice was low, almost intimate if not for the humor still present in its layered tones.

Hannah stared at him, her body taut and resistant except for the wild flutter racing through her insides. "Just do it," she whispered. She glanced away from him to study the grain pattern in the wood paneling on the wall beside her. "Quickly, please."

"Is it your right or left leg?" he inquired casually, as though he did this sort of thing all the time.

"Right," she answered with a tight jaw.

Rather than raising her skirts as she had done and as she expected, he reached beneath the embroidered hem. Hannah felt the lightest brush of his fingers over the delicate bones of her ankle before he moved his warm palm up the curve of her calf. Hannah pressed her tongue firmly against the back of her teeth, resisting the urge to jump out of his reach.

It was disconcerting in the oddest way to have a gentleman kneeling at her side, reaching beneath her skirts while she just stood there allowing it.

She must have lost her mind.

His touch was self-assured and unhurried as he wrapped his hand around her leg. The tips of his fingers tickled a sensitive spot behind her knee and Hannah instinctively pulled away. It was only a very slight movement, but it was enough for the garter to twist so sharply a small sound of pain escaped her throat.

If not for his firm grip around her knee, she likely would have stumbled.

"Easy, sweetheart. Almost there."

His voice was soothing, as though he spoke to a skittish horse.

On one level, Hannah rejected the patronizing tone as righteous pride rose in her chest. But on another level, a deeper and more visceral level, the tactic worked and she felt her muscles softening. Of course, the fact that he moved his hands over her limb with such gentle pressure and tantalizing confidence may also have contributed to the easing of tension in her body.

As he smoothed his hand higher, she felt a teasing brush against the bare skin of her thigh, causing gooseflesh to spread over her body. In the very next second, pain flared where the clasp of her garter caught her flesh.

He paused his tactile exploration the moment she drew in the swift breath.

"It seems this task will require some visualization," he explained.

"Drat," Hannah muttered before she could stop herself. She had gone this far, may as well see it through. "Just get it done, please."

She kept her gaze trained on the wall as she felt him lift her skirts with his free hand. The air against her silk-clad legs sent a delicate shiver across her skin. She wondered if other young ladies making their London debut had to suffer such humiliating indignities.

Likely not.

Such a thing seemed specifically suited for her.

Just one of the many ridiculous *faux pas* she had committed since arriving in England two years ago. Except this was a little different in that she knew the impropriety of allowing a man to touch her in such a way, let alone view her nearly naked limbs.

If anyone should find out…

Maybe she would be sent back to her parents?

The possibility had merit.

Hannah winced as he probed around the clasp with gentle pressure. Though he was obviously trying to be careful, his touch still increased her discomfort tenfold. Hannah tightened her hands into fists, distracting herself with the pain of her fingernails cutting into her palms.

"I must say, you are in possession of a gorgeous pair of legs."

Hannah gasped at his crude compliment and whipped her head about to glare at him for the blatant indelicacy. He took that exact moment to grasp her garter and give a swift tug.

Pain flashed brightly and then—relief. She was freed.

Her breath expelled in a whoosh as she twisted her upper body to glance down at the back of her thigh. She could just barely see his hands still wrapped around her leg and a purple mark forming above the spot where his thumbs pressed firmly.

"You will have a nasty bruise and the skin was punctured a bit, but you should heal fine." He glanced up at her from beneath thick lashes, his emerald-green eyes flashing with wickedness. "Is there anything else you require while I am at your service?"

The mischief in his gaze went straight to her center. "No, that is quite enough."

Hannah stepped out of his reach as he straightened to his full height. Her muslin skirts floated down to the floor, repairing her modesty. She would have liked to walk off without another word but had to acknowledge she still did not know how to get back to the grand hall. Too much time had already been spent for her to waste another minute.

She turned back to her erstwhile savior. He stood leaning one shoulder against the wall while he pulled on his gloves. His casual posture and the tilted little half-smile curling his lips grated on her nerves, but Hannah was a reasonable person.

"Would you perhaps be able to point me back in the direction of the party?" She kept her tone cool and aloof.

He arched a single black brow. "What? I do not even earn a *thank you* for my assistance?"

Hannah narrowed her gaze. "Thank you."

"My pleasure," he replied.

Though his stance was relaxed and his expression too amused to be considered seductive, Hannah felt his implication in the very tone of his voice.

"I will find my own way," she said sharply as she turned and walked away.

His low laughter followed her into the longer hallway before he called after her.

"Take the second left, then another left just past the ancient tapestry, then a right when you come to the dead end. You will reach your destination."

Hannah kept walking. She considered ignoring his instruction out of pitiful spite. But the thought of her uncle's anger should he notice her delay had her deciding to take the rogue's word for it.

His direction proved valuable as less than five minutes later, she heaved a sigh of relief when she found herself back in the grand hall.

CHAPTER 2

Miles Reginald Whitely could not put his finger on just what it was about the woman that kept drawing his interest. Despite himself, he glanced her way yet again, tilting his head in consideration as he studied her from beneath his brows.

She was passably pretty, he supposed, with her pale-blonde hair and fresh complexion. Though he stood too far to see the exact color of her eyes at that moment, from their earlier interaction he knew they were a light shade of blue. She was of average height with a figure that was fashionably slim. Modest-sized breasts pressed against her beaded bodice and the fall of her muslin skirts draped over gently curved hips.

Nothing mouth-watering there.

Yet he could not stop looking at her.

He was starting to annoy himself.

Of course, there was the fact that barely an hour before he had had his hands around her bare thigh—and a lovely thigh it was.

Miles had caressed many a female beneath her skirts. His interaction with this particular lady had not been specifically amorous. Still, he could admit to himself that the shapely lines of her legs and the subtle catches of her breath as he'd moved his hands over her bare skin had certainly put him in a sensual state of mind.

Miles understood sexual attraction, and though that was certainly present as he gazed at the unknown blonde, he acknowledged there was something else besides...

He had noticed it the moment she had glanced up and dropped her skirts in the corridor. A sizzle in the air. An odd unbalancing within him.

He felt it now as he observed her from across the drawing room, not particularly caring if his inordinate interest was noticed by the other guests.

She was dressed in the virginal white of a debutante, as so many other ladies present tonight. But there was something in her manner that set her apart from the crowd. She did not twitter like other young women. Even during their tantalizingly intimate interaction, which could have easily sent another maiden into hysterics, this one had remained calm and resolute.

While he stared, a well-dressed lady approached the blonde. As the two of them spoke, Miles noticed something else.

All of England was experiencing an unusually hot summer, and the country party at which they were in attendance was crowded with guests anxious to escape the oppressive stuffiness of town. But even the northern county of Lancashire sweltered in the heat wave. The drawing room in particular, when filled with so many bodies, had become nearly suffocating.

While the blonde's companion whipped her open fan in front of her face with so much gusto it threatened to blow over the fern behind her, the blonde remained composed. Her fan was unused, dangling by a cord around her wrist.

Miles took a quick glance about the room but already knew what he would see. Various colored fans in vibrant hues and pastels flitted and flapped about the room like a mass of frantic butterflies. He saw faces flushed from the heat and the heavy stillness of the crowded room. He saw gentlemen with moisture beading on their skin and soaking into their collars.

He looked back to the blonde. Cool as a cucumber.

Miles grinned. Interesting.

While the lady beside her continued to prattle on, the cool blonde angled her head to cast a practically disinterested glance about the room.

Though it was likely because he was so blatantly staring, Miles preferred to believe it was his striking attractiveness that drew her attention.

The moment her gaze fell on him, a jolt of lust shot through his system.

Rather than glancing away with a blush, as a well-mannered innocent should, she returned his stare with an openly assessing one of her own. Surely, she recognized him as her champion from earlier. Miles wasn't sure what he expected from her by way of acknowledgement, but when she gave just a curious quirk of her eyebrows before glancing away with a dismissive expression, amusement spread through him in a delightful rush.

Elbowing the man beside him, Miles asked, "Who is that young lady over there?"

Lord Grimm, one of Miles's best friends since Eton, flinched from the jab but craned his neck to peer through the crowd in the direction of Miles's nod.

"Eh?" Grimm squinted his eyes and then looked back to Miles with a perplexed expression, which did not worry Miles in the least since Grimm often wore a perplexed expression.

"Are you feeling up to snuff, Whitely?"

"Of course. Who is she?"

Grimm eyed him oddly and answered, but he slowed his words as if worried Miles might not catch their meaning. "That is Lady Esther, the one Father decided on for my wife. Don't you remember I introduced you to her not thirty minutes ago?" Grimm flung his arm out in a gesture to encompass the room. "She is the entire reason for this wretched party. Father wanted to put on a proper show for both our families before announcing the engagement. I swear, I explained this all to you."

Miles blinked at the enormity of his friend's error. "Of course I recall the introduction. I am talking about the other young lady. The one talking to your betrothed."

"Oh, right. Of course." Grimm peered back across the drawing room. "Let's see. That is Miss Walpole. Twenty years old. Family hails from Oxfordshire originally. She has no brothers or sisters and is being presented under the patronage of her uncle, Lord Tremaine." Grimm leaned to the side and muttered beneath his breath, "He is one of Father's cronies and a more pious man I have never met. Despite their connection, Father made it clear he expected me to stay clear of Miss Walpole."

Miles arched a brow. "What threat could the young woman possibly present?"

"Her dowry is hefty, but Miss Walpole hails from an *eccentric* branch of the family tree." He hissed the descriptor like a curse.

"How so?" Miles asked, glancing back to the young lady under discussion. She still stood near Lady Esther, but another young woman had joined them. It appeared to him the newcomer was casting rather sly glances at Miss Walpole.

"Her parents are explorers."

"Pardon me?" Miles glanced back at Grimm, wondering if he should ask his friend to speak slower again. Surely, Miles had misunderstood him.

Grimm shrugged his sloped shoulders. "You know—Egyptian pyramids, remote deserts, lost treasure, that sort of thing."

"But if the girl was raised by her uncle—"

"She wasn't," Grimm interrupted. "They say she was born in the heat of the Sahara desert and traveled all around the African continent with her parents up until just a couple years ago." He squinted his eyes and curled his lips distastefully. "In truth, she seems a bit odd, if I do say so. Even her cousins avoid a great deal of association with her."

As Miles observed further, Lady Esther and the other lady made their excuses and strolled away, leaving poor Miss Walpole standing by her lonesome. A veritable wallflower.

She did not look particularly awkward. In fact, she looked rather content to stand by herself observing her surroundings.

Still, Miles felt it his duty as a gentleman to rescue the poor thing, especially if she did not even have the sophistication to realize she was on the verge of appearing to be a social pariah.

"I want an introduction," he declared to Grimm.

His friend groaned. "Dammit, Whitely. Why her? I haven't even been properly introduced to the girl."

"Then find someone who has, because I intend to meet her."

Grimm groaned again, but he acquiesced. Grimm always acquiesced. His father had made sure to bully any resistance out of the poor man ages ago.

While Grimm craned his neck this way and that, scanning the room for someone who could make the proper introduction, Miles decided he didn't want to wait. He took off in a purposeful stride across the drawing room.

HANNAH SAW HIM COMING. She just did not believe his audacity.

That he would dare to stare at her so openly through the crowd was shocking enough, not to mention annoying. But that he would dare to approach her with his bold grin was quite uncalled for. She knew it because her uncle had spent the last twenty months ensuring she fully understood the expectations of *polite* society.

She wasn't sure what prompted the green-eyed demigod to alter his direct course as he neared, but she watched him covertly from the corner of her eye as he sidled around through the crowd to her right before getting lost from view.

She tensed, sensing his pursuit was not at an end but unsure where he might next appear. And so it was when she finally heard his low murmured voice just behind her, she barely managed to contain a startled jump.

"Enjoying yourself, Miss Walpole?"

Hannah squared her shoulders and sent a forced-casual gaze out over the drawing room.

"You should not speak to me, my lord. We have not been properly introduced."

"I know." He sighed dramatically. "It is a shameful situation, which is why I have got someone seeking out a means to obtain an introduction at this very moment. In the meantime, since I am already here and we are already talking, how about an improper introduction. I am—"

"I know who you are," Hannah stated sharply. This man was clearly intent upon ignoring the rules of propriety.

"You do?" He sounded genuinely surprised.

Hannah nearly scoffed but recalled such a sound was not considered ladylike. "My cousin told me all about you, Lord Whitely. She...met you during her season two years ago. I must insist you walk away and leave me be."

There was only a brief pause before he said, "I trust you have had no further problems with your garter?"

In truth, her leg had started throbbing incessantly a few minutes after she left him. Though thanks to him, at least she could walk without wincing in pain. But she was not about to provide any of that information. The man had far too intimate knowledge of her person already. That he would bring up such a topic here in the midst of so many who might overhear convinced her even more of his lacking sense of decorum.

She responded to his question by turning her back more squarely to where he stood behind her. He could ask her inappropriate questions all he liked; she would simply ignore him.

He chuckled warmly at her reaction. The rumbling sound made her stomach tremble. The man found amusement in the oddest things.

"You wound me, Miss Walpole." His voice had gotten closer. So close she felt the waft of his breath against her nape. Hannah stiffened despite herself. "That you would treat me so shabbily after I came to your rescue."

"I have no doubt you will recover," she whispered.

"But my wound is deep. I would recover faster with your gentle touch."

"No doubt there are other women present who would be more than happy to administer to your needs."

"But I want you."

"You cannot have me."

Hannah's lungs grew tight as she felt him step closer. His legs stirred the fall of her gown, brushing them against the back of her thighs.

"I beg to differ," he whispered across the back of her neck.

Gooseflesh rose on her skin as a tingling shiver coursed down her spine, making Hannah strengthen her resolve. She needed to convince him to ply his flattery elsewhere. Against her better judgment, his whispers were starting to have an effect.

She cleared her throat. "You are wasting your efforts on me, Lord Whitely. I am unseduceable."

More laughter rolled around her, through her. Her low belly tightened.

"Is that a word?" he asked, amusement thick in his voice.

"It does not matter," she replied, "because it is true. I am more likely to convince you to marry me than you are to seduce me."

She felt him stiffen the instant she uttered the M word. A smile of triumph tugged at her mouth. It seemed she'd hit on something that might scare him off.

"I accept your challenge," he replied after a moment.

Hannah blinked in confusion. Without considering her actions, she turned to look over her shoulder at him. "Wait. That was not a challenge. It was simply a figure of speech."

"It does not matter," he said, repeating her earlier phrase with a wink, "because I have accepted."

His green eyes flashed as he gifted her with a wide and winning grin. The effects of his smile were devastating. Her breath seized and heat flooded her extremities.

"Drat," she muttered from a tight throat.

CHAPTER 3

Miles always made a point to learn as much as possible about a topic that interested him.

And Miss Walpole definitely interested him. He had not been merely flirting when he had declared he planned to seduce her. He wholeheartedly intended to do just that. And in seduction, as in any endeavor worth accomplishing, it paid to gather all available intelligence.

Over the next couple of days, Miles learned as much about Miss Walpole and her family as he could. Though, in truth, there was little known beyond what Grimm had already disclosed.

He also maintained a casual distance from the wary young woman. When one's first encounter has your hands up a lady's skirts, it was prudent to take a few steps back. He found it easy enough to place himself in her vicinity without appearing suspicious. He reveled in the occasions when it was perfectly natural to pass near her, catch her sweet scent and hear the distinct tone of her voice.

The more he refrained from indulging more significantly in Miss Walpole's company, the more he desired it.

A poignant discovery, considering he had long ago accepted his tendency to lose interest in things rather quickly despite the intense curiosity they initially sparked. With Miss Walpole, Miles faced the possibility his interest ran far deeper than mere curiosity.

Of course, she was a fascinating creature.

In his sometimes covert and sometimes blatant observation of the young lady, Miles acknowledged there was more about her that set her apart than simply her cool attitude. She had a lovely relaxed way of moving. So different from the tortured postures of other young ladies who were not long from the strict dictates of the schoolroom. Miss Walpole also had a different way of looking about her. She had a clear, intelligent gaze, and open interest. No coy looks or sly glances for her.

In all of his observations, Miles never saw her twitter or shrink. She didn't seem to know how. If she wanted to know about something, she asked.

For her part, Miss Walpole did an excellent job of avoiding any direct contact with him. However, it was the indirect that convinced Miles she was not as oblivious to him as she tried to present. It was not long before he noticed that her gaze would seek his location whenever she entered a room.

On the third day after their first meeting, Miles encountered the perfect opportunity to take his pursuit to the next level.

It was just barely past breakfast and already the day was proving to be exceptionally warm. By midday it would likely prove to be quite unbearable. Yet Grimm's father had planned a picnic in the vale past the deer run. Another option for the day was to climb into stuffy carriages for the two-hour drive to the nearest village for a meal at the inn then shopping at the local market.

The idea of sitting in the enclosed air of a carriage only to spend several hours perusing the wares of rustic craftsman before riding in said carriage back to the estate did not appeal to Miles in the least. Then again, picnicking under the hot sun did not seem like a good time either.

Miles sat on a low stone wall that jutted out from the side garden of the manor house. It was one of the few spots of shade on the east lawn. The only reason it was not occupied was because the gathering group of guests who were scattered about before him were about to set out for their picnic. The servants had left more than an hour before to set up shade tents and blankets for the ladies to sit upon. Another round of servants had followed just a few minutes ago with the food.

He had been watching all morning for the curious Miss Walpole to appear. If she had joined the group heading for the village, he would have jumped aboard her carriage despite the stifling discomfort.

Gratefully, she had not, so Miles assumed she would be down shortly as the nearly three dozen picnickers were soon to depart.

Maybe he would get lucky and she would stay behind in the house. Considering the heat, there was a chance she would opt out of both planned excursions.

He did not bother to hide the grin splitting his face at the thought of going on a merry hunt through the empty house, seeking out the cool beauty.

Alas, he was not to be so lucky, as the lady suddenly made her appearance, practically flying down the front steps of the manor, still tying her bonnet beneath her chin. The grin on his lips faltered at the unexpected jolt she gave his system. Her appearance was fresh and invigorating. She was dressed simply in a muslin gown with daffodil-yellow trim and a bright yellow sash beneath her perfect breasts.

Perfect?

Hadn't he thought them a bit small just yesterday?

He was sure he had, but seeing them now, tucked modestly behind the white virginal bodice, made his heart thud awkwardly against his ribs. She crossed the front drive in long strides as she made her way to three other young ladies.

Miles glanced away from Miss Walpole long enough to note that the group she approached consisted of her cousin, Miss Beatrice Tremaine, and two other young ladies who were making their debuts this season. Miles's inquiries had revealed that Miss Tremaine had a tendency to say some rather nasty things about her cousin.

Just before Miss Walpole reached them, Miss Tremaine leaned

toward her two friends to whisper something that had them all exchanging sly smiles.

Miles stiffened but did not move from his position beneath the apple tree, preferring to watch the scene. At least for the moment.

He was too far to hear any of the words spoken, but he was a relatively good translator of body language. As Miss Walpole reached the other young ladies, her cousin initiated a display of distress. All the ladies began to show concern and tried to comfort the girl, but it was Miss Walpole who seemed to offer a solution. Miss Tremaine appeared ever-so-grateful. Miss Walpole patted her cousin's arm in a comforting gesture before she turned away and headed swiftly back into the house.

"What the hell?" Miles muttered.

Just as Miss Walpole was fully out of sight, Miss Tremaine withdrew a handkerchief from the wrist of her glove with relish and a laugh. The other girls burst into giggles.

Miles's jaw felt tight with anger.

For the most part, he loved being around people. The many possible human foibles never ceased to amuse him, and he loved a clever conversation. But if there was one thing he abhorred, it was bullies. It was the very reason he had befriended Grimm all those years ago. That some people would choose to belittle someone for the purpose of raising themselves grated harshly on his nerves.

A moment later, a shout went up indicating it was time for the party to depart for the vale.

The gathered group of guests began to meander down the drive, following Grimm's father who led the procession on horseback. From there, they cut across the north lawn to take up the path that led them through the woods to the vale on the other side. Miss Tremaine and her friends linked arms joyfully and set out to make their way with the rest of the guests.

For how many people there were, it took a surprisingly short time for everyone to disappear into the shadowed forest.

Miles however, stayed on the wall beneath the apple tree, swinging his leg in a relaxed rhythm as he waited for the reappearance of Miss Walpole.

She did not leave him stranded for long.

Though he had just seen her not fifteen minutes earlier, the sight of her again nearly stopped his breath. Especially when her light steps faltered at realizing everyone had gone on without her. She stopped and stood looking about, a bit dumbfounded, a handkerchief pinched lightly between her fingers.

Miles jumped to his feet then and began a jaunty stroll across the lawn.

"Miss Walpole, a lovely morning, is it not?"

She looked at him, eyes wide and wary, clearly not having noticed him before that moment. But now that she had seen him, she shifted her weight back and forth, as though trying to decide if she should stay or run. Lucky for him, her indecision allowed him the time he needed to reach her side.

She tipped her head back to see him from beneath the wide rim of her bonnet.

"Lord Whitely, I had not expected to see you about so early in the day. I thought rakes and libertines preferred to stay abed past the noon hour."

"Ah, that is only when we have a delightful companion with whom to while away those pesky morning hours. And I was sadly quite alone in my bed last night."

"How terrible for you," she muttered as she shifted her gaze to scan the wood line and lane for any sign of the departed party.

"Indeed. And since you were the cause of my cold bed, I fully expect you to make it up to me."

That brought her attention swinging back to him. Her blue eyes were bright with surprise and her lovely mouth dropped open. "Wait. What?"

"It seems we both missed the group heading for the vale. Will you keep me company on the walk?"

Her gaze narrowed as she eyed him askance. "What have you done with everyone?"

"Nothing," he replied, all smiling innocence, "but I do know where they went. We should be able to catch up to them quite easily. Will you accept my escort?"

Her hesitation should have bruised his ego, but Miles found he rather liked that she did not trip over herself for the opportunity to be alone with him. Many young ladies would have. Many young ladies had at some point or another in the past.

She glanced down at the handkerchief in her hand. He suspected she knew her cousin had sabotaged her and was not surprised by it. Issuing a sound somewhere between a sigh and harrumph, she tucked the white scrap of linen into her sash before replying.

"I cannot imagine they have much of a start on us. I accept your offer, Lord Whitely, but do not expect me to take your arm."

Miles smiled. "I will accept those terms. But keep in mind, should you trip over a tree root or slip over uneven ground, you will be entirely on your own."

A reluctant smile crinkled the corner of her mouth. Miles found his attention captured by the sight of it.

"Do not worry about me, my lord. I managed an eight-day trek through the foothills of the Simien Mountains without a gentleman's steadying hand, and all while carrying a heavy pack on my back and leading a stubborn mule. I daresay I can manage the wilds of Lancashire." She glanced about. "So which way did they go then? Down that path there?" she asked, pointing at the narrow lane heading into the forest.

"No," Miles answered more abruptly than he intended, having been thrown off by her unexpected rejoinder.

She glanced at him in confusion. "Isn't the picnic spot located beyond the deer run?"

"Yes, but there is a more scenic route than through the woods. This way," he said as he gestured back across the lawn.

Though he had visited this estate a number of times with Grimm, they had not exactly been interested in taking walks about the estate. Miles truly had no idea whether the direction he planned to take was more scenic or not, he just knew it was opposite of the way the others had taken.

"Let us be off then," she said as she took off in long, purposeful strides. "Lead the way, Lord Whitely."

Miles allowed himself just a moment to admire the view of her departure before jogging to catch up to her.

CHAPTER 4

It really was a lovely day. So unlike what Hannah had gotten used to since coming to England. She had not seen nearly enough sunshine in the last couple years. She wished she could toss her bonnet aside and feel the warmth on her bare head.

But such behavior would be frightfully unseemly, and she could not risk any stragglers from the party ahead of them catching a glimpse of her in such a state. In thinking of the others, Hannah lifted her gaze to scan the path ahead. She and Lord Whitely had been walking for nearly fifteen minutes at a pretty good pace, surely they should have met up with members of the other group by now?

Then again, he had said they were taking a scenic route…

She glanced at the ridiculously handsome lord strolling along beside her. She sincerely hoped this wasn't some trick to get her alone. He had been fairly quiet so far, no inappropriate flirtation or attempts at unnecessary touching. Basically, none of the sorts of things she would have expected from someone who had declared he planned to seduce her.

But then she knew very little of such things. Maybe the English thought of seduction in very different terms than what she imagined.

In truth, the renowned scoundrel had been rather circumspect over the last couple days. If she were a trusting sort, she would have thought he had changed his mind about pursuing her. But she was not so foolish to dismiss those times she had caught him watching her—and it had been often enough—with a quiet little grin barely hiding on his lips.

It did not bode well that his attention, however brief or covert, managed to warm her as intensely as the desert sun. In fact, it was quite aggravating since Hannah knew full well nothing would come of it. Nothing could.

As though sensing he was the focus of her thoughts, Lord Whitely slid his gaze to the side and gave her a wide grin and a wink.

She told herself it was the fact that she had begun thinking of seduction that had her insides dissolving in delicate tingles. But she knew it was him—and his flashing green eyes—that had her twisted up so neatly.

Her oldest cousin, Jacqueline, had been so very right to bemoan her acquaintance with this man. Though Beatrice had often called her sister silly, Hannah could easily see how Lord Whitely had managed to ruin Jacqueline during her cousin's first season two years ago. It should have been Hannah's first season as well, had her uncle not decided she needed more training in the areas of decorum and deportment before he would allow her out in society as a representative of their family.

If Hannah had had access to her own money, she would have purchased a ticket back to Africa many months ago, though by now, her parents had likely moved on to another location. They rarely stayed anywhere for very long. As it was, her uncle held her purse on short strings. He had been burdened with the task of seeing her settled into a proper English marriage and that was what he would do. Whether Hannah wanted the same or not.

"Did you really climb a mountain carrying a pack on your back and leading a mule?" Lord Whitely asked, bringing her back to the present moment.

Her uncle would prefer that no one know how she had lived before coming to England, but Hannah did not like lying. Besides, she saw nothing wrong with the life she'd lived with her parents.

She gave a short nod. "It was just the foothills, but, yes, I did."

"Fascinating," he replied.

He didn't seem particularly shocked by her admission. Anyone else who learned of her unusual upbringing tended to stare at her as though she had just admitted to being from another planet.

"I almost think you mean that," she said.

"I do," he answered as he lengthened his stride to step in front of her and turn around to continue their conversation face-to-face while he walked backwards. "I imagine you have done many things that would astound the average Englishman. I would love to hear more."

Hannah was conflicted. Was it a ploy?

Likely so, but she didn't really care just now. The sun was shining, reminding her vaguely of home. And for the moment anyway, she and the puckish scoundrel grinning at her were the only people about. She could almost pretend they were not smack dab in the middle of the dreary English countryside.

"You do not find me odd?" she asked with an impish smirk of her own.

"Certainly," he answered. "That's exactly what I find fascinating. The moment I saw you lift your skirts, I knew you were not the typical sort of lady."

Hannah narrowed her gaze and pursed her lips to keep from laughing. He certainly had a way of lightening the tone. "I imagine you thought me an easy mark."

The laughter faltered in his bright green eyes. Instead of answering, he swung around again to fall into step beside her. The shift in his demeanor was almost startling.

"I am not everything they say about me, you know."

Hannah considered what she had heard. "Hmmm. You mean you are not a conscienceless flirt and indiscriminate seducer of innocents and sophisticates alike?"

"Would you believe me if I said I had absolutely nothing to do with the women who claim to have been ruined by me?"

"Not at all," she replied without a second thought.

"Do not get me wrong. I enjoy a rousing flirtation." He tossed her a wink. "But I have not done half the things people have claimed."

"I admit I find that hard to believe."

He shrugged. "For the most part, I enjoy the notoriety. It is amusing to see what people will believe about you with no actual proof. But for some reason, I would rather you know the truth."

Hannah couldn't be sure he wasn't just saying what he thought she'd like to hear.

"Which is…?" she prompted, curious about him despite herself.

"I am not the scoundrel and libertine everyone makes me out as."

"Hmm," she responded with a noncommittal sound.

He laughed. "I can see you are unconvinced. I suppose I should not be surprised."

They lapsed into a sort of uneasy silence for several minutes as the terrain they walked tilted upward and grew rocky and uneven enough that some concentration was required.

After Lord Whitely assisted her with climbing over several groupings of boulders, which she honestly could have leapt over far easier on her own, she finally paused to ask him, "Are you sure we are heading in the right direction?"

Her hand was still in his after he had hoisted her to the top of a particularly large outcropping of rock. His other hand rested on the small of her back. It was a rather inappropriate position, she realized now that she took a moment to think about it. Of course, she had the excuse that she was unaccustomed to all the rules and limitations regarding casual physical contact amongst men and women of the upper classes. Such would not be his excuse, however.

"Most definitely," he replied with a hearty grin.

Hannah knew she should pull away, her uncle's voice in the back of her mind screamed at her for her loose manner.

But Whitely's eyes were so blasted green, and his hand at her back and the other holding hers were so warm and strong. And his lips were a ridiculously pleasant shape, as were his shoulders and legs and hands and face. Everything about him was quite agreeable, actually.

Not just his appearance, which in truth was a few steps beyond such a mediocre adjective, but also the way he talked to her. Like she was a real person.

As they stood there, balanced together on the top of the rock, she felt suddenly lightheaded and confused.

"Do you hear water?"

Hannah blinked.

He turned and squinted into the sun, throwing his face into sharp profile. She found herself distracted by the line of his jaw and the shape of his ear.

"Yes, I see it. Come on."

Without warning, he jumped to the ground and clasped his hands around her waist to lift her down after him. Then he clutched her hand in his as he practically dragged her along the trail, twisting around more rocks and leaping ditches formed by water running from the higher ground.

Hannah couldn't help but laugh at his obvious enthusiasm. She grasped her skirts to lift them out of the way as she leapt agilely after him.

"Where on earth are you leading me?" she questioned good-naturedly. "What did you see?"

"This," he answered as he stopped and pulled her up alongside him.

Hannah followed his sparkling gaze to the stunning sight of a crystalline pool of water trapped by a formation of boulders and fed by a stream of water tumbling down a rock wall. The water reflected the bright sunshine with watercolor hues of blue, green, and gold. It was picture perfect.

"What on earth," she murmured as she stepped closer to the edge. The pool was quite deep and big enough to hold perhaps five men comfortably. The water, so clear and bright, looked unbelievably refreshing.

She glanced around them and realized for the first time that they had been slowly making their way up into the hills. The path going back the way they had come sloped slowly downward and the path ahead only went up. She didn't recall anyone mentioning such an incline on the way to the picnic spot.

A forest-green coat dropped to the rocks at her side. With a start, she turned to see Lord Whitely unbuttoning the front of his waistcoat.

"What are you doing?" she exclaimed.

His grin was boyish and naughty. "I am going for a swim."

He tossed the waistcoat aside and bent over to pull off his boots.

A flash of panic seared through Hannah. *This* was certainly not appropriate.

"No, you are not. Someone from the party may come back this way and see you."

He shrugged and continued to strip off his stockings and then went for his neck clothe. Stopping finally as he stood in nothing but his buckskin breeches and thin white shirt, he turned and gave her grin.

"Won't you join me? I cannot imagine it is so deep you won't be able to touch the bottom." He wriggled his brows suggestively. "Though if it is, I won't mind if you wish to cling to me for safety."

"You are not really going in," she insisted. Of course he wouldn't.

He just lifted his brows and stepped up to the edge. Before she could say a word to stop him, he made one long leap.

Hannah gasped as cold water splashed back at her.

He resurfaced with a shake of his head and a wily grin.

"Come on then. The sun is hot and the water is cool. It feels amazing. You know you want to," he challenged.

"Not a chance," she said, holding back a smile. The man had no boundaries to his behavior. "My uncle would throttle me. He may still if someone catches me talking to you like this. I am sure this is breaking at least a dozen rules."

"No one is going to come this way," he assured calmly. "You are entirely safe from censure, I promise."

Something in his confident tone struck a note of caution in her mind. "How can you be so sure?" Before he could speak, she answered her own question. "We are not following the party, are we?"

His expression was unrepentant and just a little self-satisfied. "No."

"You *are* a scoundrel," she accused.

"Listen," he said as he swam forward to the edge of the pool, basically to her feet. "No one will ever know we came up this way together. Not unless you tell them. So why don't you simply enjoy the unexpected respite and take advantage of this slice of paradise?"

Hannah did not answer right away. The man had a valid point. And the water did look heavenly. She used to swim a lot before coming to England, before she was advised such frolicking was reserved for children.

But, no. She could not risk it.

She glanced away from him.

"Fine," he said, a stubborn tone coloring his voice. "I will just stay submerged until you change your mind."

Hannah glanced back at him just in time to see him pushing off from the rocks to fall back under the surface with a rolling splash. She shook her head at his antics. Did he really think to convince her with that?

She crossed her arms over her chest as the rippling water stilled over him. It was clear enough to see his wavering form sitting on the bottom of the pool.

How long had he been down there? Twenty seconds maybe?

Another ten went by, then twenty more on top of that.

Hannah untied her bonnet and set it on a rock beside his coat. How long could a man hold his breath? She kicked off her shoes. Thirty seconds to a minute on average, perhaps? She had once seen a pearl diver off the coast of Persia hold his breath for four minutes easily. But that had been accomplished after years of training.

Lord Whitely was a pampered Englishman.

And he had already been underwater for nearly two minutes.

"Drat," she muttered as she reached for the back of her gown and pulled the buttons free with a rough yank and tug, sending several bouncing down onto the rocks. "I am going to have to save him."

CHAPTER 5

Hannah gasped as the water closed around her. It was a great deal colder than she'd expected. Holding back her panic, she kicked off the rock wall and dove toward his wavering image.

The water was not very deep and she reached him in seconds.

As soon as she grasped the front of his shirt, he brought his arms up around her and propelled them both toward the surface in a rush.

She blinked the water from her eyes. Opening them wide, she found herself staring directly into his ridiculously handsome face, which was split with an engaging grin.

"I knew you could not resist."

"Bloody hell," she whispered. "You're mad."

He just smiled bigger and arched his winged black brows. "Were you attempting to rescue me?"

Feeling exceeding disconcerted, not only by the realization he had not been in any danger at all, which was astounding, but also by the fact that he continued to hold her against him in a way that had them pressed to each other from chest to knee. His arms were tight enough around her middle that she was lifted off the floor of the natural pool while the water lapped just below her breasts.

Planting the heels of her hands against his shoulders, she exerted some pressure.

He didn't budge.

"Admit it," he said, narrowing his gaze to strips of vivid green.

She did not miss how his voice lowered to a warm drawl. Nor did she miss how the muscled shape of his shoulders felt hard like marble yet far from cold beneath her hands. Nor could she possibly ignore the heat that seeped from his body into hers even while the water swirled frigidly around them.

"You were devastated by the thought I might expire down there alone in the murky depths."

Hannah executed a gentle eye-roll at his last statement. "This pool is hardly murky. And how on earth did you manage to stay down there so long without breath?"

He shrugged, and the movement caused an interesting friction against the peaks of her breasts.

Hannah shook off the delightful sensation.

"When I was six years old, I got a cramp while swimming in the pond on our estate and couldn't get to the surface. My older brother saw me thrashing about and rescued me, but I discovered I rather enjoyed the attention I garnered from my brush with death. Mother was so rattled she did not allow me back to the pond the rest of the year. I spent my time practicing how to hold my breath, extending the time I could resist the urge to inhale. When the next summer came along, I played a little prank on my siblings." His smile turned naughty and Hannah's heart took a little dive. "They didn't think it was nearly as funny as I did."

"I imagine not," she chided. "That is a terrible prank."

"I learned early that in order to be noticed in a family the size of mine, one often needed to go to extremes."

That explained a lot. "Just how large is your family?"

"Ridiculously large."

"How ridiculous?" She was curious despite herself.

"I grew up with one older brother, four younger, and five bright and beautiful sisters."

"That is amazing." To an only child, the numbers were simply astounding.

"Yes, well. Sadly, against my parents' wishes, my older brother insisted on going to war on the Continent. He did not return."

"I am sorry. That must have been difficult for your family."

He issued a sigh. "It was. It still is, to be honest. But life finds a way to continue on and my youngest sister was born less than a year after his death. She was a bit unexpected." He gave a wide grin. "My parents are still very active, you could say."

"Oh goodness, I would rather you didn't."

"Why? Does the idea of procreation make you nervous?" His tone was light and joking, but he still hadn't loosened his inappropriate embrace.

And she had long since stopped trying to get him to.

"Of course not," she replied honestly. "It is a natural occurrence in the animal kingdom. For all our airs as human beings, we are far more animalistic than we would like to admit. We have simply learned to disguise our instincts behind manners, or we have forgotten them altogether in the hopes of distancing ourselves from the natural world." She sighed, thinking of her life before England. "It is rather sad really."

"You are a source of unending astonishment."

Hannah studied his face for evidence of ridicule. "Don't you mean amusement?"

She gave another push at his shoulders. He shrugged and finally loosened his hold enough for her to step back.

"Sure," he agreed. "Amusement as well. But then I try to find amusement in just about everything."

Hannah did not doubt him. She already knew his humor was as much a part of his personality as his penchant for flirtation. She lifted her hands to push back strands of her hair that had fallen from her coiffure to drip on her face. As she did so, she watched his gaze fall to her breasts.

She glanced down at herself. Now that he wasn't holding her

against him, the front of her body was quite exposed. The thin muslin of her chemise was soaked and had become entirely transparent.

Too late, she recalled that the British tended to be rather uncomfortable with openly displaying the natural state of the human body. To Hannah, who was familiar with having to bathe in public rivers and other watering holes when necessary, such forced sensibilities seemed a bit unnecessary. Not to mention contradictory when ladies of the *beau monde* had been known to dampen their skirts to display their charms more clearly, or rouged their nipples to make them more obvious.

Lowering her arms, but refusing to cover herself despite the bold admiration in his gaze, she tipped her head to say sardonically, "I know how people look at me." Her words brought his gaze back to meet her eyes. "They think me strange and find it enjoyable to make subtle little digs against my background or my respectability or what have you."

She sighed, and although his gaze flickered, she admired that he kept it on her face.

"Frankly. I do not care what most people think."

He smiled then. A low and widening grin that lit his whole face. "Bravo. You shouldn't. And neither do I. Unless their opinions make me laugh, which they often do. Then I might be guilty of encouraging them."

Hannah laughed. She couldn't help it.

"Oh ho," he exclaimed in mock surprise. "She laughs! Perhaps Miss Walpole is capable of having fun after all."

Hannah threw him a spirited glare but couldn't keep her lips from curling upward. "Can I help it if I find this country repressive and dull?"

He snorted. "Darling, we all find it repressive and dull. That is why I claim my joy wherever I can."

Without warning, he dove under the water. Hannah had only a second to step back and gasp a breath before he wrapped his hands around her ankles and pulled her under. He released her once her head submerged and she used her momentum to twist around him as he rose back to the surface. By the time she came up for air, she was directly behind him, and without thought of decorum, she reared up and grasped his shoulders as she threw her weight to the side. Effectively dunking the much larger man.

She did not need to think about the propriety of her behavior because she knew quite well it was not done for young ladies to engage in any kind of horseplay, let alone with a man while in the water and barely clothed. But she didn't give a damn. Somewhere in the last few minutes, she had decided to take his advice and seize the unexpected respite she had been gifted with that morning.

Though she'd managed that one bit of surprise, he had amazingly quick reflexes and was exceptionally agile in the water, nearly as agile as she was herself. In the end, his strength won out over her quickness and they both came up for air with his arms once again secured around her body. Only this time, he held her aloft against his chest. One of his arms wrapped around her back and the other beneath her legs.

She had nowhere to go.

Laughing, she pushed her sodden hair out of her face, the full length having long since fallen from the elaborate style her cousin's maid had created that morning.

"All right, Lord Whitely, I accede this skirmish to you. You have earned your victory."

He shook his head like a dog, his thick black locks sending water flying everywhere.

Hannah laughed again and wrapped her arms around his neck as she closed her eyes to await the end of his final assault.

"Won't you call me Miles?" he asked once he had finished.

Hannah opened her eyes and her gaze slammed hard into his bright green eyes. Water dripped from his thick black lashes and ran down the side of his handsome face from his temples, over his strong cheekbones to his angled jaw.

Wet and disheveled, he looked more like a man than a demigod. Stripped of the fine high-society veneer, he was even more dangerous than Hannah could ever had anticipated. Because in his current state, she got a glimpse of who he truly was—a flesh and blood man with a grin that made her knees weak and eyes that saw her as she was beneath the layers of her uncle's reformation.

His smiled widened when she said nothing, as though he understood her sudden distraction. Which was really rather annoying once she considered it.

"I think our relationship has extended past stiff formalities, don't you?" he asked again.

"We have no relationship," she replied, needing to create some distance, in theory, if not in physical actuality.

"Not yet." He lowered his tone. "I have to admit to being a little disappointed in your efforts to convince me to marry you, or rather, lack thereof. It makes me think you might not be taking this challenge seriously enough."

This time, Hannah snorted. "You would be right. I am most certainly not taking your silly challenge seriously." She squirmed in his hold, trying to signal to him that she wished to be released. Instead, he shifted his hold beneath her legs to grasp her more securely around her thighs. She narrowed her gaze but continued, "I have no desire to wed you, Lord Whitely."

"You forfeit already? Wonderful!" he exclaimed. "Seduction it is then."

"No," Hannah denied quickly, though heat flashed through her blood at his words. "I told you I will not be seduced and I meant it."

His smile curved into a very masculine depiction of satisfaction and triumph. The expression made Hannah's toes curl and her stomach flutter distractingly. Then he tipped his head toward her until his mouth was just a breath away from hers.

Hannah could only stare into his eyes. They had darkened around the edges so that only a ring around the center remained vivid green.

"I have already seduced you, Hannah. You are just too stubborn to admit it."

And then he kissed her.

Boldly. And with a little growl in the back of his throat that went right through Hannah's resistance like lightning through the night sky.

AMY SANDAS

Her resistance would have been token and futile anyway.

The instant his mouth touched hers, Hannah knew he was right. She was seduced. From the moment he had crouched beside her to free her garter and grinned up at her with his devilish gaze to ask if she required anything else.

When she responded to his kiss with a tightening of her arms around his neck and a shift of her shoulders that pressed her breasts to his chest, he flicked his tongue past her teeth.

Hannah gasped. That small invasion sparked a conflagration throughout her body.

She opened to him and twisted in his hold, seeking some deeper connection.

With another bold and delicious sweep of his tongue, he shifted his arms. Keeping one arm around her shoulders, he released her legs, which allowed her to form the front of her body against the hard planes of his chest and abdomen. The heat of him was startling and consuming, especially when she felt the hard, hot ridge of his erection against her trembling belly.

She held him tighter, loving the way his large hand palmed her right buttock, kneading and forming her flesh with strong fingers.

She also loved the taste of him, so masculine, unrestrained, and erotic.

She did not realize he had been moving her through the water until her back came up against the rock wall of the pool, worn smooth by ages of water lapping at its surface.

Trapped between the rock at her back and the insistently sensual man at her front, Hannah broke from the kiss to draw a desperate breath.

He did not let up his assault and lowered his mouth to her throat. Gripping her buttocks in both hands, he lifted her against him. Her legs parted naturally around his hips as her breasts came nearly level with his face.

"Ah," he said raggedly, his warm breath bathing her collarbone just before he dipped his chin to draw the hardened tip of one breast deep into the hot cavern of his mouth. The thin layer of her soaked chemise was no barrier against the dance of his wicked tongue over her nipple.

Again, the contrast between his body heat and the chill of her skin roused sensations that strained for expression. She wrapped her arms around his head, cradling him to her breast as she tightened her thighs around his hips.

Suddenly, she sympathized with all the young ladies who had come before her to be ruined so thoroughly by this man.

Just as quickly as that thought formed, another followed in its wake.

She did not want to be another in a long line of his conquests.

With immense reluctance, she released her hold about his head and shoulders. She brought her legs down along his.

He did not cease the assault of his mouth, even when he tightened his hands on her rear in resistance to her retreat. She eased her hands against his shoulders. This time, he did not ignore her.

He lifted his head with a low growl and allowed her body to slide down his until her toes met the sandy bottom of the pool.

Looking into her eyes with his emerald gaze, he offered a gentle smile.

"Too much?" he asked with a quirk of his brow.

She gave a stiff nod. "Quite."

"You realize this has only just begun," he said.

"Begun and ended, my lord," Hannah said with conviction. Now that she knew how far he was willing to go—how far *she* had been willing to go—she was not going to allow anything like this happen again.

"Are you certain?"

She tensed at the sardonic confidence in his tone, but she was not able to prepare her resistance when he lifted his hands to cradle her face and brought his mouth to hers once more.

Against her will, she arched into him, tipping her head back against the rock to allow him full access. As he staked his claim over the deep recesses of her mouth, coaxing her tongue into play, Hannah curled her hands into fists in the wet material of his shirt. A moan reverberated from her chest.

When he finally ended the kiss, she said nothing. Just opened her eyes and flattened her hands again to give a solid shove.

He stepped back and she dove swiftly to the side. She swam across the pool in long strokes until she reached the spot where she had dropped her clothes.

Without glancing back at him, she pulled herself from the pool and began the process of wringing the excess water from her chemise and hair before drawing her dry gown over the top. Hopefully, the sun would remain strong on the walk back to the house, allowing any remaining moisture to dry up. For her hair, she finger-combed it and then braided its length before coiling it atop her head and tucking in the end. With the bonnet replaced, no one would know it was not how she had worn it earlier.

She refused to glance back at Lord Whitely even though she suspected quite strongly by the heat traveling over her skin that he watched her rather intently.

Only when she sat on a nearby rock to replace her shoes did she lift her gaze to him.

He stood where she had left him, his arms crossed over his chest, his mouth—the sight of which sent tingles through her low belly—curved into a careless grin.

"I have got you, Hannah. There is no getting out of this."

She assumed he meant his vow to seduce her.

Standing with her head high, she allowed her gaze to travel over the parts of him she so admired. His handsome face, broad masculine shoulders, and muscled arms. She even took a moment to direct her gaze to a point beneath the surface of the water where she suspected he burned for her still, just as she did in the hollow, aching place between her thighs.

Then she met his gaze again, accepting the desire she saw there. Accepting her own desire that ran like fire through her bloodstream.

Smiling, she said, "I am already out. Turn your attention to some other young woman. You will not have me."

Without waiting for his reply, she turned and strolled back down the path the way they had come.

Miles waited until she was out of sight and then took a massive breath and dunked beneath the water. He did not come back up until his lungs burned and his head grew fuzzy.

And when he did break the surface, it was with a raw curse. "Bloody fucking hell. I'm a goner."

Then he burst into full-throated laughter.

CHAPTER 6

The next evening was an elaborate dinner party with a guest list that extended to local gentry. Two long tables were set up in the dining room and were crammed with diners seated elbow to elbow. Miles was disappointed to find that Hannah had been placed at the opposite table nearly the full length of the room away. It made for a very dull dinner.

By the time the gentlemen finished their port and cigars and joined the ladies in the drawing room, his target was fully ensconced within a gaggle of ladies. That she was already peering across the room at him suggested she had been watching and waiting for his reappearance. That he detected a distinct light of triumph in her gaze, told him she had infiltrated the close-knit group with the express intention of thwarting his attention.

Poor girl, he thought as he made a beeline for her position. If she expected a handful of females would deter him, she had no idea who she was up against.

Her gaze darkened and her expression faltered as she realized his intention. Her traitorous cousin, who was seated beside her, looked up as well and noted his approach. Miss Tremaine said something in an aside to her two friends, who in turn peeked at him from beneath coyly sweeping lashes.

Miles recognized the look. The one innocents sent his way all too often. More so once rumors had started to spread that he had a penchant for ruination.

He didn't.

In fact, he had never given any undue attention to an innocent in his life. But once one wayward debutante had made the unfounded accusation several years ago, others followed suit. Miles became the go-to scapegoat for young ladies who needed an excuse to get married and quickly. Of course, there were also those women who earnestly sought his attention, hoping for an exciting dalliance. Such had been the case with Miss Walpole's older cousin, Jacqueline. That one had been relentless in her insistence they commence an affair. Miles had never been interested in the woman. When she'd finally accepted that fact, she'd thought to force the issue by insisting he had seduced her.

Lucky for Miles, her father had absolutely no intention of giving his precious daughter to a scoundrel. Instead, Lord Tremaine had her married off to a very proper and staid example of manhood.

Miles rather enjoyed the false reputation he had built up. He had fun with the notoriety and the persona it gave him. Never mind that when it came to romance he was much more circumspect. One could even say he was downright traditional. Oh, he was a flirt to be sure. But he never pursued a woman who did not know exactly what to expect from him.

That is, until Miss Walpole.

He supposed he should take some time to consider what that might mean.

But not just now, as he finally reached the group of females forming an unintentional barrier between him and his current objective.

"Ladies," he said with a winning grin, addressing them all at once. "I wonder if I might borrow Miss Walpole for a moment. I understand she has significant knowledge on a topic with which I find myself rather fascinated." Finally focusing on her directly, he asked, "Miss Walpole, would you take a turn about the room with me?"

She was going to refuse. He could see it in her stern chin and her lowered brows. Just as she parted her beautiful lips to speak, her cousin piped up with a hard smile.

"Of course. She would be delighted. Wouldn't you, dear?" she insisted with an obvious elbow jab to Hannah's ribs.

To her credit, Hannah did not flinch, though Miss Tremaine's elbow looked sharp indeed. Instead, she paused to glance at the other ladies present and, as though realizing she was quite cornered, gave a weighted sigh. "I would be honored, my lord."

Miles grinned at her flat tone.

The gaggle parted to allow her to step through their midst. Miss Tremaine gave a parting jab, though this one was with her tongue. "I must admit I am rather curious as to what my cousin could have knowledge of that anyone, least of all a gentleman of your caliber, Lord Whitely, would find fascinating."

Hannah had just reached him as her cousin spoke. He gallantly offered his arm. She slid her hand into the crook of his elbow and he looked into her blue eyes. He couldn't resist the answer that slipped from his mouth.

"Oh, I would have thought it obvious," he said with a grin, never looking away from the lady at his side. "It is Miss Walpole I find fascinating."

And with that he led her away. The sound of gasps and twitters following in their wake.

"Was that really necessary?" she asked coolly.

"Definitely." He slid her a sideways glance and noted the slight tinge of pink in her cheeks and the tension around her mouth, a dead giveaway that she held back a smile. "Admit it," he challenged, "you enjoy that I shocked them just a bit."

She lowered her gaze for a second before she replied. "I do appreciate anything that manages to leave Beatrice speechless, if even for a moment."

"Too bad it could not be longer."

She stifled a laugh behind her glove.

"That is uncharitable. My cousin has been nothing but gracious since her father took me in."

"You are a terrible liar."

"I know."

"Then why don't you stop lying to yourself and admit you want me in your bed."

"I do not," she snapped in quick reply.

"My bed then. It makes no difference to me."

She stumbled and he took advantage by drawing her more closely to his side. That she did not step away from him once she had regained her balance pleased him in no small manner. In fact, it made him quite warm inside.

No. Hot was a better word for it.

Acknowledging his rising lust, Miles directed them toward the windows lining the far side of the drawing room. They had all been thrown wide open in an attempt to draw in a cooling breeze. Unfortunately, even the nights were exceptionally warm, and whatever breeze could be had was more balmy than cooling.

It did nothing to ease the steady fire building beneath the surface of his skin.

"You will keep lying to yourself then?" he asked in earnest.

"I never lie to myself."

The tone of her voice struck a chord deep within him, forcing him to stop. He took her hand in his and drew her around to face him. Her lovely features were firm and resistant, but her gaze met his unflinchingly.

"So you acknowledge you want me." It was stated as fact.

She did not deny it. Just lifted her chin a notch higher. She was so beautiful. Her gaze held such strength and confidence. He truly admired that about her. She knew herself and trusted herself. All others be damned.

"Yet you continue to deny us both," he stated in a private tone.

"I must."

"Why?"

"I will not be seduced."

"Why?" he prodded again.

She turned her head to look out through the window. "I think too much of myself to become another one of Lord Whitely's ruined castoffs."

Miles kept his focus on her profile. "I told you I am not the reprobate everyone claims."

She rolled her gaze back to him. "No doubt you swore the same to each of the ladies you ruined. I am not so gullible."

For the first time, Miles realized the downside to years of false rumors and implied indiscretions. He felt himself growing angry that she would refuse to take his word for it. Then realized he couldn't blame her for doing exactly what everyone else was doing.

"Ah, what a blasted coil," he lamented.

She smiled at his dramatic response and shook her head gently. "You should really just turn your attention elsewhere, Lord Whitely. It will save us both unnecessary trouble."

"I tend to enjoy trouble," he rejoined with a wink. "Yours especially since it occasionally leads to broad glimpses of your stunning anatomy."

She gave him a swat on the arm and his words tumbled into laughter. She glanced around to be sure no one was close enough to hear his improper remark.

Looking at him with a narrowed gaze that made her blue eyes flash with annoyance and something else, she said, "Nothing happened. Nothing is going to happen. Now let up on this nonexistent challenge and leave me be."

"Can't," he replied with a grin. "Not until I win."

She took two long, steady breaths as they stared at each other. Each of them taking the other's measure. Neither of them anticipating their opponent's surrender, nor truly wanting it.

Then she issued the sigh of a woman tortured by the persistent idiocy of the male species.

Miles had heard the sigh a thousand times before from his sisters and had learned long ago there were two ways to counter female annoyance—humor and honesty.

"You are relentless," she accused.

"And you are the most fascinating woman I have ever met."

"Then you must know a frighteningly dull selection of females. That or you are a recluse." She tossed him a cheeky glance. "Perhaps the rumors about you are as false as you claim."

"Of course they are. Still, I happen to know some very interesting and attractive women. You surpass them all."

She shook her head in amusement. "Your flattery is impossible to believe when it goes so far, my lord."

"It is not flattery when it is true, Miss Walpole. You should know how much I admire you."

"You desire me. There is a difference," she retorted.

"There is," he agreed, "and I do both. I am rather talented in that way."

She snorted back a laugh as another strolling couple passed near their spot. Once the semblance of privacy was restored, she gave him an assessing glance. "You are an accomplished flirt, I will give you that."

"And an excellent kisser."

Her eyes widened fractionally. After a breath, she replied in a low voice, "Yes. Inspired actually."

"A passionate lover," his murmured.

The pulse at the base of her throat fluttered and her gaze darkened. "There are more important things than passion."

"Impossible," he countered with a heavy brow. "Name one."

"Constancy. Trust." She paused. "Love."

Miles grimaced. "I said one."

"Take your pick," she said with a wave of her hand.

"No, thank you. I have decided to be greedy. I choose all of them."

Her mouth was open, ready to retort, when her delightful cousin sidled up beside them. Miles coughed back a sound of irritation as he saw that Miss Tremaine was accompanied by Lord Hathmore, a man with more self-righteous condemnation than any Miles had ever met. The bloke thought himself a saint of the highest order, when he was nothing more than an uptight prig.

"The two of you look frightfully cozy over here in the corner by yourselves," Miss Tremaine said with a sly smile. Then she leaned toward Hannah to whisper *sotto voce*, "Do be careful not to let father spy you so *intimately* engaged with Lord Whitely."

Though Miles noted a slight stiffening of her shoulders, Hannah tipped her head and replied in a light tone, "Your concern is appreciated, but we are hardly *intimately* engaged. Surely, there can be no fault observed in a conversation."

"If I may say, Miss Walpole," Lord Hathmore intruded, his beady eyes darting to Miles before looking back to Hannah with an earnest sigh, "that all depends upon who is involved. In this case—" his censorious glance slid once again toward Miles, "—you have cause to heed your cousin's words."

Miles gave a jaunty bow as though accepting a compliment, but Hannah gasped in mock astonishment. She even brought her hand swiftly to her breast. Miles hid his grin at her theatrics. What a delightful creature.

"My goodness! Lord Whitely—" she leaned toward him with her eyes round, "—did you know you were such a scoundrel?"

"Indeed. I can ruin a lady with just a look." He glanced toward Miss Tremaine, casting her a smile heavily tainted with wickedness.

The silly twit fluttered before she gathered her composure to say to Hannah, "Do not say I did not warn you, dear cousin. All it takes is one inappropriate move and you will be ruined." After she spoke, Miss Tremaine's pinched face slid into a disturbing smile. She looked back and forth between Miles and Hannah and then tapped Lord Hathmore's arm with her fan. "I have done what I could. Let us move on."

As they walked away, Miles looked back to Hannah. Her expression of amusement slid immediately into one of weary frustration.

He dipped his head toward hers. "What is the matter?"

"I feel like I am trapped in a perpetual game where the rules keep changing."

"Then make your own rules."

"To what end?"

Miles smiled. "That all depends on what you want."

Her blue eyes looked at him, so clear and vivid, as she seemed to think on his last comment. Then she shook her head. "If you will excuse me, Lord Whitely."

She turned and walked away, leaving him standing there with an ache in his chest that felt an awful lot like loss.

CHAPTER 7

Hannah claimed the first opportunity she came across to retire early that night. She occasionally felt Lord Whitely watching her after their stroll, but she refused to glance his way again. The man had managed to make her already conflicted feelings even more complicated.

She had come to England to please her parents. They felt it important once she reached marriageable age that she have the opportunity to meet proper English gentlemen. Hannah had known the moment she was first presented to her uncle that she would not be the success her parents envisioned. But she had been determined to do her duty and experience a full Season before returning home. After only a few weeks, she wondered why she'd even bothered.

Her debut was a dismal failure.

And now, she also had the disconcerting attention of Lord Whitely to contend with.

The more she tried to ignore him, the less she wanted to. Although a great deal of her internal conflict came from the rather intense physical attraction she felt for the man, the rest had to do with the fact that she was coming to appreciate his humor, his easy manner and the way he made her feel. She was more relaxed and like herself in his company than she had been in the last two years.

After changing into a lawn nightdress and brushing the length of her hair, Hannah stretched out on her bed. Her thoughts were in turmoil over the feelings she was developing for a very improper gentleman, but the night was warm and deep. Sleep claimed her with little effort.

It could not have been much later when Hannah was abruptly brought back into full wakefulness. Tension slid along her limbs, but she did not alter the pattern of her breath nor move a muscle beyond a tightening of her hand beneath her pillow. Something had stirred her from her sleep. She was just not sure yet what it was.

She listened for a moment. There it was again, a light scratching at the door and a murmured, "Hannah."

It sounded like Beatrice.

Hannah swept from the bed and went quickly to open her bedroom door. Her cousin stood in the hall, still dressed in her evening gown and wringing her hands as though she would twist them off.

"Oh, thank goodness, Hannah, you have to help me," she muttered while her eyes darted desperately down the hall.

"Beatrice, what is it?"

Her cousin keened softly. "Something awful. Just dreadful. I need your help."

The woman was distressed beyond reason. "Come in, Beatrice," Hannah replied in an even tone, hoping to calm her. "We will talk about it. I am sure whatever it is, there is a reasonable solution."

"No!" Beatrice reached out to wrap her long fingers around Hannah's wrist. "You have to come with me. Immediately."

She began to tug violently on Hannah's arm.

"Wait, I must fetch a robe."

"No time," Beatrice insisted, choking on a sob. "It is just horrible. Please, you have to help me."

Alarmed at her cousin's odd behavior, Hannah allowed herself to be pulled down the hallway, hoping they were just going to her cousin's bedroom.

They were not.

Beatrice kept a death grip around Hannah's wrist as she tugged her all the way down the hall to a servant's stairway at the back of the house. Down they went to the ground floor, Beatrice shushing Hannah every time she tried to question what had happened or where they were going.

They continued along a narrow, darkened corridor, one that looked similar to the one Hannah had gotten lost in the night she'd met Lord Whitely. Hannah rushed along behind Beatrice, her bare feet making barely a sound. Wearing only her nightdress with her hair falling free down her back, she was grateful for the lack of light as they made their way past a series of rooms that opened off the corridor. She had no idea if it was late enough to assume everyone was asleep and sent a silent wish that they would not have the misfortune to encounter anyone.

A faint glow could be seen up ahead, signaling the end of the corridor. Beatrice stopped in front of a room several paces from the reach of light. She finally released Hannah's hand and pointed into the unlit room.

"There. You have to see for yourself."

Hannah couldn't help but be suspicious of her cousin's motives. Beatrice had not exactly been a friend to her since she arrived in England. But as she glanced at her cousin's pale face, nearly twitching in her anxiety, she knew she would have to at least take a look. She could not imagine it was anything truly awful.

"Are you coming with me?" she asked.

Beatrice shook her head and backed away, saying in a quivering whisper, "I cannot."

Hannah nearly rolled her eyes, but she knew that if she were ever to get back to her bed, she was going to have to play this out.

Hannah entered the room. A pair of tall windows allowed the faintest shimmer of moonlight into the space. Since Hannah's eyes were already accustomed to the darkness, it was more than enough to see that she was in a sort of music room. She scanned the shadows for some evidence of what had so distressed Beatrice. All was silent and still, with nothing seemingly out of the ordinary. Certainly, nothing that could have caused such a panic in her cousin.

To be sure, Hannah decided to make a full circle of the room before returning to Beatrice to ease her cousin's mind and find out specifically what had roused the other woman's fright.

Just as she came around the piano set in the far corner, she sensed a shift in the room. She looked back toward the doorway and stopped suddenly at the sight of Lord Whitely.

Tilting her head, Hannah scowled. "What on earth…?"

He came forward, and though Hannah's skin tingled and the hairs on her arms rose, it was not from fear. Rather it was the sort of magnetic attraction she had come to expect whenever in the company of this man.

"What are you doing here?" she asked in a harsh whisper.

His steps hesitated and his open expression shifted into one of bewilderment. "What do you mean? You sent me a note, asking me to meet you."

She shook her head. "No, I did not," she muttered. The truth hit Hannah like a searing arrow to her center. "Beatrice."

What trouble had her cousin concocted now?

Hannah rushed forward, intending to brush past Lord Whitely to confront her cousin, who had conveniently disappeared.

He caught her arm at the last moment, drawing her to an abrupt stop at his side. "Wait. Listen," he whispered into her ear.

Hannah ignored the way contact with his body sent a shiver of pleasure through her. Now was not the time to allow her wayward desire to interfere. Blocking the sound of her swiftly beating heart, she finally detected the murmur of approaching voices and recognized her uncle's heavy tone.

She looked up at Lord Whitely, panic infusing her blood, urging her to run. His gaze was trained on the open doorway, the muscles of his jaw repeatedly clenched and released.

The voices neared and Hannah heard her uncle say, "I do not appreciate this rude interruption, Beatrice. What could you possibly have to show me?"

"You will see, Papa," Beatrice replied with a rushed urgency.

Hannah could picture her deceptive cousin trying to rush Lord Tremaine down the hall. But Hannah's uncle was not easily manipulated. He would be walking with his typical sedate pace regardless of Beatrice's urging.

Hannah's gaze darted about. There may still be time for her to get out of this.

If she could just find a place to hide.

Whitely tightened his hand around her arm as he stepped around to face her. "Hannah," he whispered.

Something in his voice sent a shiver through her center. She pushed her hair back from her face and looked up to meet his eyes. She had never seen him with such a serious expression. Her heart stopped.

"It is too late," he murmured just as Hannah's uncle stepped into the doorway.

"What is the meaning of this?" he bellowed. "Hannah?"

She could not move. She knew exactly what her uncle saw. A young woman, barely dressed, standing in intimate proximity with a man known for seducing innocents. Her stomach twisted. Beatrice had warned her, hadn't she?

Anger and frustration clutched at her.

"Step away from my niece, Lord Whitely."

He did, but not before he whipped off his coat and drew it around Hannah's shoulders to provide her with at least that bit of modesty. She automatically gripped the lapels to hold the coat secure. It still held the warmth of his body and carried the essence of his scent. For some reason, that gave her a reminder of herself.

She would not be cowed by this moment.

Another of her father's rules came to mind. *When disaster strikes, as it sometime must, remain unbroken. Calmly assess the damage, make a plan, and then execute it.*

As Whitely stepped back, she turned to face her uncle. She refused to allow her gaze to drift even momentarily toward Beatrice, who hovered behind her father.

Hannah had no idea her cousin was such an accomplished actress.

Lifting her chin, Hannah waited for her uncle to speak.

"Go with Beatrice back to your room. You are not to leave, do you understand? I will speak with you in the morning."

"Yes, Uncle."

Hannah walked past him into the hallway. She refused to acknowledge her cousin as she strode swiftly down the narrow hall to the stairs she and Beatrice had come down only minutes earlier. But Beatrice would not be ignored. She fairly danced along beside her. Finally, Hannah could take no more. "Why?" she asked bluntly.

"You never should have made your debut during *my* season. Do you have any idea how annoying it is to be constantly known for having such an odd cousin? You are all anyone talks about. It has been dreadful."

"So you sought to ruin me?" Hannah asked, incredulous over how someone could be so devious.

"Oh, you were doing that already on your own, dear cousin. I simply hastened the inevitable end. Whitely of course will refuse to do the honorable thing as he has so many times before. And you will be married off to some poor sop willing to take damaged goods. I will have the rest of the season to myself. It is perfect."

They had reached Hannah's bedroom. She couldn't hold in the anger frothing beneath the surface any longer. She turned and met Beatrice's smug grin.

"Beatrice, you are a bitch," she said simply before she closed the door in her cousin's outraged face.

The crude insult gave her some satisfaction, but not nearly enough. Stalking across her bedroom, she tossed Whitely's coat onto her bed and lit some candles.

She was not going to stick around to be humiliated by some forced sense of morality when she had done absolutely nothing wrong.

She stalked to the wardrobe, pulled out an armful of gowns and dropped them on the bed next to the borrowed coat. Then she stomped over to her luggage trunk, which had gratefully been left in a corner of the room. She grabbed the leather handle on one end, hauled it out and began tossing her gowns in one at a time.

She would need to get a servant's help to carry the thing downstairs once it was packed. And she would need to ask for the use of a carriage to take her to the village. She had some pocket money. Hopefully, it would be enough to buy a seat on a coach traveling to London. Once there, she would have to visit her uncle's solicitor if she were to obtain the funds for passage on a ship leaving England.

That may prove to be difficult if her uncle refused to release the money, but she would deal with that obstacle when and if she reached it.

She never should have allowed her parents to convince her to come to England. It had been a disaster from day one. Tonight proved it. She did not belong here.

Hannah whipped around the room, collecting her possessions and tossing them into the trunk. In her irritation, she was unmindful of their care. Her only thought was on getting the task done and now.

"You will never get everything to fit if you continue to pack like that."

At the sound of Whitely's voice, Hannah spun around with a startled jump.

He had somehow managed to enter her room and close the door behind him without her notice. Seeing him in her bedroom—still in his evening wear sans coat, his mouth curved in amusement, his eyes so vividly green they seemed for a moment to light the room—Hannah acknowledged once again her fierce attraction for him. It was strong enough to distract her from her current purpose. Potent enough to slice through her anger.

The tension suddenly released from her shoulders and spine,

making her slouch. She dropped the hairbrush she had been holding into the trunk before pushing the wild fall of her hair back over her shoulders.

"What do you want?" she asked.

"Me? Oh, I just came for my coat," he answered with a casual swagger as he walked toward her.

Hannah watched him, the emotions that had been crowding her chest now tightening in her belly. "You should not be here."

He arched his brows. "Afraid I'll ruin you?"

She laughed. It was a nervous laugh that did nothing to ease the wash of awareness claiming her. It was as if all her anger and disappointment took a sharp turn in his presence. The heat coursing through her now had nothing to do with her previous frustration.

"Yes," she admitted. "I suppose that ship has sailed, hasn't it?" She lifted her chin. "What did you say to my uncle?"

"Not much. It is you I would prefer to talk to."

"Does he know you are here?"

"No."

He had been slowly approaching her as they spoke. As he answered her last question, his attention dipped below her chin. Wonderfully intricate sensations trickled through her body in reaction to the change in his expression and the intent light that entered his gaze.

The ties at the neck of her lawn nightdress had loosened while she had been flying about the room. The gown had slid off her shoulder to catch on the upper swell of her breast.

She remained still as stone while he lifted his hand.

For a second, it seemed he would replace the gown where it had slipped from her shoulder, but the moment his fingers brushed her bare skin, he appeared to change his mind.

He wrapped his hand around her upper arm and the warmth of his touch soaked into her skin, heating her flesh. When he swept the pad of his broad thumb over her bare shoulder, a tingling shiver rolled down her spine.

He lifted his gaze back to hers.

She knew exactly what he was thinking, what he was feeling. Because she felt the same thing. Hannah took a shallow breath through parted lips and made a decision she never thought she would make. Before she left England, she was going to have him in her bed. Tonight. Right now.

CHAPTER 8

Stepping up to him, she lifted her hands to slide them up over the satin surface of his waistcoat. The heat of his body seeped through the material, warming her palms. She recalled from their swim how tautly muscled his chest and abdomen had felt against her body, and she tested those muscles now with the exploration of her fingers. Reaching up to curl her hands over his shoulders, she rose onto her tiptoes and tipped her head back.

Their mouths were a breath apart. His eyes were sharp and alert beneath the dark sweep of his lashes. Hannah's stomach fluttered in anticipation of his kiss.

But he made her wait. He lifted his hands and combed his fingers back through her hair at her temples. Fisting his fingers gently at the back of her scalp, he finally lowered his head.

Despite his primitive grip in her hair, the touch of his lips was soft as a butterfly's wings. He brushed his mouth across hers with infinite patience. Barely caressing the surface, making her ache for a deeper connection.

Hannah leaned into him and wrapped her arms around his neck, drawing him to her.

With a chuckle sounding in the back of his throat, he bent down and looped his arm around her legs to lift her against his chest. He continued to press heated kisses to her mouth while he strode to the bed. After laying her down, he stepped back to quickly strip off his waistcoat and kick off his shoes.

Hannah watched his disrobing with interest. When he had stripped in similar fashion at the hidden pool, she had been too irritated to enjoy the unveiling of such a well-formed physique.

Noticing her avid gaze, Miles grinned. The smile was pure sensuality and sent a jolt of desire through her core. With the grace and poise of a man who knew he was attractive, he slowed his movements. He lifted his shirt up over his head and tossed it to the floor.

Naked to the waist, he gave Hannah another wicked glance and struck a dramatic pose that flexed his muscles to their greatest definition.

Hannah laughed at his antics even as she admired the sculpted ridges and shadows of his body. He seemed to know just how to keep any situation from turning the corner into something overtly serious.

Her laughter died abruptly as he joined her on the bed, settling his weight intimately atop her. She gasped and then sighed as her body accustomed itself to the sensation of his large male form pressing her into the mattress. One of his legs rested between hers and he held himself up on his elbows to look down into her face.

"Are you sure you want this, Hannah?"

The earnest tone of his voice surprised her. If she answered no, he would leave. She knew it, and her heart swelled almost painfully. For all his roguish posturing, he had a noble soul. She realized then that she had always known it, had simply been afraid to trust what her instincts told her about him when it seemed to contradict what everyone else insisted was true.

"I want you, Miles." Then she pursed her lips in a rueful smile. "It looks like you won the challenge after all."

His grin was charmingly lopsided as he lowered his head toward hers. "Not exactly."

"What do you mean?"

"Stop talking," he murmured against her lips.

And she did, because he had shifted his leg to press more intimately to the juncture of her thighs. His erection was hard and insistent against her hip. He swept his tongue into her mouth and its velvety glide sent her senses spinning.

She arched up into him, seeking the press of his chest against her breasts.

No. She wanted more than that. She wanted to feel his body beneath her hands.

She planted her foot against the mattress and pushed at him, angling him off to the side. He resisted at first, but when she nipped at his lips with her teeth, he acquiesced with a short laugh. As he rolled onto his back, she followed, rising over him. Sitting beside him, resting on one hip, she looked down at his outstretched form. The muscles of his arms, chest and abdomen were more defined than she had expected. She lifted her hand to trail a light touch over the contours of his body.

At her first exploratory caress, he propped his hands behind his head, essentially giving her free rein. Hannah met his hooded gaze and smiled, feeling a sudden rush of sensual power at having such a man lying patiently in wait for her to satisfy her curiosity. Holding his gaze, she circled the flat discs of his masculine nipples. She delighted in how they puckered to small points against the pad of her index finger while gooseflesh rose on his skin.

As if sensing her enjoyment, he chuckled low in his throat.

Emboldened, she trailed her hand up over the bulge of one biceps and leaned forward to flick her tongue against his nipple. His chuckle slid into a swiftly drawn breath. The planes of his stomach tightened visibly, drawing Hannah's attention. She shifted to press a kiss just below his lowest rib.

His breath caught.

She ran the tip of her tongue down the center of his abdomen to his navel.

He exhaled with a whoosh.

Sitting tall again, Hannah eyed the obvious ridge of his desire still concealed by his breeches. Without hesitation, she released the fastenings, wanting nothing more than to see him, touch him. His erection came free, reaching up along his belly. Hannah tugged his breeches lower until Miles lifted his hips to allow her to pull them down his thighs. From there, he used his feet to kick them the rest of the way off.

Hannah sat back, running her gaze over his body finally revealed in its entirety. He was stunning. Purely male. She had seen men in various forms of undress before. African natives who did not have the same need for modesty as the western world. But never had she been so affected by the sight of male anatomy.

Her mouth was suddenly dry and her fingertips buzzed. Deep inside, melting heat overtook her, bringing a throbbing wetness to the juncture of her thighs. She pressed her legs together and rolled her lips in between her teeth.

As she looked her fill, gazing intently at all the ways he was formed so differently from her, he lay there still but not relaxed. His muscles tensed and twitched as her gaze passed over them. And when she allowed herself the pleasure of observing his erection, she noticed how it throbbed and pulsed against his belly. How it impossibly appeared to grow even more while she watched it.

"Touch me, Hannah," he said. His voice was strangled and tight.

Hannah glanced up to see his jaw clenched so hard it looked like marble and his eyes locked fiercely on her face.

"Touch me," he repeated.

Hannah lifted her hand to run just the tip of her finger up his length, from the base to tip. He was hot and smooth. She circled her finger around the ridged head and then teased the small slitted opening, causing moisture to seep in the wake of her finger. Curious, she ran her thumb through the droplet, spreading the silken issue over his tip.

The muscles of his buttocks clenched as he lifted his hips, as though trying to press himself more fully into her hand.

Hannah laughed softly but gave him what he wanted and wrapped her fingers around him.

He groaned.

She squeezed.

He tensed his buttocks again, thrusting himself against her palm. She slid her hand along his length, reveling in the satiny glide of his hard flesh as she wondered what it would feel like when that part of him entered her body. She was a virgin, but she knew well enough the act of procreation. The thought of experiencing such an intimate joining with Miles made her tremble. The throbbing between her legs increased to an insistent ache.

As though understanding the craving that claimed her, he gave up his submissive posture and wrapped his hand around the back of her neck to draw her mouth to his. She tumbled forward onto his chest and fell into the kiss. He brought his other hand to cup her buttocks, rolling her more fully onto him until his cock thrust up against the softness of her belly.

His kiss became deeper and more penetrating. She groaned into his mouth as he kneaded her derriere.

With a growl, he lifted and rolled, taking her over until he was atop her once again. This time, he settled both legs between hers, forcing her thighs to widen around him. Her nightdress was twisted up around her hips and she gasped as the hot, smooth tip of him pressed to the entrance of her body. But he did not push forward. Instead, he lifted his shoulders until he could grasp the neckline of her gown. He tugged it down, exposing her breasts to his view and the possession of his mouth.

He circled each thrusting peak with his velvety tongue, scraped her softness with his teeth and drew her deep into the heat of his mouth. Hannah clasped his head in her hands, holding him to her breasts as she rolled her hips beneath him, craving the awkward pressure and friction it caused. Needing more of it.

But instead of giving her what her body demanded, he lifted his hips away.

Hannah protested with a low sound in the back of her throat. He murmured a soothing sound before he reached down and slid his fingers along the seam of her needful flesh.

Hannah jerked and arched.

He teased and coaxed her by turns. Stroking her with his long fingers, then circling, then flicking and rubbing before starting all again. Every second ignited more fire in her blood, urging the ache to a restless hunger. And then the first intrusion into her body. A gentle press of his finger easing along her inner flesh. Then a second finger and the initiation of a rhythm that tormented beyond reason.

Hannah was lost. Her panting breath, her clutching fingers, her rocking hips, all belonged to a woman possessed beyond reality. She had not expected such intensity, such a feeling of being consumed.

It was not until she was completely mindless that he pressed his hips between her thighs once again. And now, finally, what she had been striving for. The steady pressure of his erection spread her, claiming her with slow, intense strength. Her body stretched, her need grew until that moment of inner resistance.

Miles looked into her eyes then, his green gaze darkened by desire, his brows low and his breath coming fast between his lips. So much restraint. So much focus.

And all of it for her.

Hannah wrapped her arms around his neck and flicked her tongue over his lower lip. He released a guttural groan as his hips jerked forward to press more painfully to her core. Hannah stiffened from the searing burn, but before he could retreat, she lifted her head to thrust her tongue deep into his mouth. When his tongue met hers, she closed her lips over it, sucking it into her mouth.

He thrust his hips forward with enough force to tear through her maidenhead as he filled her completely. Miles dropped his forehead to hers. His breath was fast and stilted as he held himself still inside her.

But Hannah was out of patience. Even the burn of her lost virginity could not keep her from moving, grinding herself against him as she sought his mouth again. The pain was nothing compared to her need.

Propping himself on his elbows, he framed her face in his hands and kissed her. Deeply. Tenderly. She may have considered it reverent if not for the carnal taste on his tongue and the wicked heat of his breath.

Hannah soaked up that tenderness. She drew it into her body through his breath and claimed it as rightfully hers. And suddenly, she knew. This was far more than an expression of physical lust. Her inevitable joining with this man had far deeper implications than that of desire. As she lay beneath him, his body penetrating hers, his weight all around her, she acknowledged her own vulnerability.

She had let him into her body and into her heart.

For the life of her, she could find no reason to regret it. Every instinct she possessed urged her to accept it as a gift. Regardless of what may come after. This moment, with this man was entirely worth it.

After a few long, wonderful minutes, his kiss grew more potent. He started to move within her. First, there was a slow withdrawal. Then an even slower repossession. He would not be rushed as they moved together. Soothing, tormenting. Building the tension.

Their panting turned to groans and gasps. Their sweat mingled.

The pleasure took Hannah steadily higher and higher. Until a moment of breathless suspension when everything stopped. Her thoughts, her breath, her heartbeat. And then the most sublime expression of life she had ever experienced washed through her on a wave of intense sensation. No minute corner in her body was left untouched or unchanged. And she clung to Miles, her mouth pressed in an open kiss to his shoulder, trusting him to carry her through.

Two more languorous thrusts and he joined her. His spine arched and a groan caught in his throat as he ground his hips to hers. Hannah lifted her knees along his sides and grasped his buttocks in her hands, urging him to go as deep as he could.

CHAPTER 9

Miles released his breath in a heavy whoosh. He barely managed to shift his weight before he collapsed to the mattress along Hannah's side. Stretching an arm over his head, he dislodged the pillows on the bed and something heavy clamored to the floor.

Hannah emitted an unintelligible sound but did not move from her sated sprawl beside him. He cast a long look at the woman who lay mostly naked, her skin still flushed, her pale hair a tangled mess beneath her head, her eyes gently closed while her breath slid from between parted swollen lips.

Miles's heart was near to bursting. It was an exceptional feeling and he struggled to contain the emotion pressing outward against his rib cage.

Unable to keep from touching her, he covered her breast with his hand. As the steady beat of her heart echoed against his palm, warmth spiked in his chest. He took a moment to revel in the sensation, understanding and delighting in what it signified.

Then his curiosity got the better of him. He gathered the strength to lift himself up to stretch across Hannah's lovely body until he could gaze down over the edge of the bed.

Amusement washed through him as he reached for the fallen object. Propping himself on one elbow, he examined it with a mix of curiosity and bewilderment.

"Do you always sleep with a dagger beneath your pillow?"

She gave a heavy sigh and opened her eyes in a sleepy gaze. "Since I was five years old. A necessary defense against predators that hunt in the night."

Miles couldn't help himself. He burst into laughter. Without a doubt, this woman was the most adorable, fascinating, wonderful creature he had ever met. A wrinkle formed between her brows as his laughter continued and he leaned forward to press a kiss to the little frown.

Lifting his head, he muttered through a wide grin, "I love you."

He did not realize he had said the words aloud until her eyes blinked wide open, the haze of her sensual aftermath gone in an instant. She took a breath in obvious preparation to protest.

Miles had to act fast. He pressed his fingers to her mouth. "Before you say anything, I have a confession. I did not come to your room tonight to fetch my coat. I had an ulterior motive."

She pushed his hand away to reply in a wry tone. "I think our current circumstances prove that well enough."

Miles couldn't help but grin, considering the circumstances she referred to included him lying naked half atop her flushed body. "An added bonus," he quipped, "but my true purpose was to discuss what will be expected after tonight."

She slid her gaze away from his face. "You do not have to explain. I understand. I am leaving England as soon as I can. You will not have to worry about…any of this. None of it will matter once I am gone."

The idea of her leaving England burned his insides like a red-hot lump of coal. But he had come to her room tonight prepared to say goodbye if that was what she wanted.

Could he really do it? Be that selfless?

He groaned and rolled his eyes closed.

Damn it. For her happiness, he would do that and more.

"Honestly, Miles," she said in a lowered tone. "You do not have to marry me."

"You are correct," he said almost angrily as he opened his eyes again. "I do not have to, and if you insist, I will pen a note to your uncle rescinding the offer I made downstairs and will ride away from here before dawn."

Her blue gaze was wide and locked on his. In their clear depths, he thought he saw a touch of the fear he felt himself. The fear and the longing.

He drew a ragged breath and framed her face in his hands. He brushed his thumbs over the crests of her cheekbones before pressing them to the pulse at her temples.

"Hannah," he said, "I *want* to marry you. I cannot imagine a day without you in it, let alone the rest of my life. Please stay in England. Stay and become my wife."

She stared up at him in silence for several long seconds. Then she swallowed and licked her lips. "How many other women have you claimed to love?"

Miles's stomach tightened. "None. I swear it."

She arched and imperious brow. "And how many have you proposed to so eloquently?"

He knew then she was only tormenting him. He issued a growl and wrapped his arm around her waist. He gave a rough tug and pulled her to lie atop him until her pale hair fell about them like a curtain. With her lovely hips in his hands and her breasts swelling beautifully beneath his chin, Miles found it difficult to form a proper response, but he gave it a valiant effort.

"There has never been and never will be another woman to ever hear those words from me."

But her gaze was still skeptical. "You have known me less than a week. How could you possibly love me?"

Miles shrugged. "I am not one to question the hows and whys of things. I trust what I feel. Can you?"

She stared down at him with her beautiful blue eyes. She would not be rushed, he knew, but Miles tensed with every second that passed. If she refused him...

When she finally spoke, it was in the tone of someone reciting a phrase from memory. *"When embarking on any journey, having companions you trust is vital, but not nearly as important as trusting your own intuition."*

Miles arched his brows in question.

She smiled and lowered her lips until they hovered just above his.

"I trust you, Miles, and I trust what I feel," she whispered, repeating his words.

"And?" he prompted as he ran his hands up her narrow spine.

She laughed, a soft and lovely sound. "I love you."

He wrapped his arms around her, holding her close as her lips continued to tease his by barely brushing back and forth over the surface.

"And?" he muttered as his pulse picked up speed.

"I will be your wife." Her breath bathed his lips, and the taste of her response was sweet indeed.

Miles sighed his relief. She sealed her vow with a kiss, but as it gradually grew deeper and more impassioned, he abruptly pulled back, thinking of one last thing.

"You must promise not to tell anyone I agreed to this marriage willingly. I cannot have my false reputation ruined with the truth."

Her laughter this time was a full throaty sound that vibrated up through her chest to surround him in a delightful sense of rightness. Without even trying, she had claimed his heart. The world would think Lord Whitely, renowned for ruining young innocents, had finally chosen the wrong woman to seduce and was going to find himself at the alter whether he liked it or not.

In truth, Hannah was the only woman Miles had ever set out to seduce, and he could not be more thrilled to have won such a bride.

ALSO BY AMY SANDAS

PERIL & PERSUASION
Noble Scoundrel

Tender Blackguard

RUNAWAY BRIDES SERIES
The Gunslinger's Vow

The Cowboy's Honor

The Outlaw's Heart

FALLEN LADIES SERIES
Luck is No Lady

The Untouchable Earl

Lord of Lies

REGENCY ROGUES SERIES
Rogue Countess

Reckless Viscount

Rebel Marquess

Relentless Lord

Regency Rogues Box Set

REFORMED RAKES NOVELLA SERIES

Wicked

Dangerous

Brazen

Reformed Rakes Box Set

STAND-ALONE TITLES

Kiss Me, Macrae

ANTHOLOGIES

Christmas in a Cowboy's Arms

Longing for a Cowboy Christmas

ABOUT THE AUTHOR

Amy writes historical romance about dashing, and sometimes dangerous, men who know just how to get what they want and women who at times may be reckless, bold, and unconventional, but who always have the courage to embrace all that life and love have to offer.

Amy grew up in a small dairy town in northern Wisconsin and after earning a Liberal Arts degree from the University of Minnesota - Twin Cities, she eventually made her way back to Wisconsin (though to a slightly larger town) and lives there with her husband and three children. She spends her days writing and the rest of her time trying to keep up with the kids and squeeze in some stolen moments with her husband.

You can find Amy on her website http://www.amysandas.com/
On Facebook at https://www.facebook.com/AmySandas?ref=hl
Or follow Amy's tweets at https://twitter.com/#!/AmySandas

Manufactured by Amazon.ca
Bolton, ON